The Little Pony

With thanks to Dido Fisher for information about ponies

Edited by Gillian Doherty   Additional design by Sam Chandler

First published in 2008 by Usborne Publishing Ltd, 83-85 Saffron Hill, London EC1N 8RT, England.
www.usborne.com First published in America in 2009. UE. Printed in Dubai.

The Little Pony

Anna Milbourne

Illustrated by Alessandra Roberti

Designed by Laura Parker

Down at the stable,
something wonderful has happened.

A new foal has been born.

"What shall we call him?" asks little Rosie.
"Let's call him Pepper," says her brother Tom.

Pepper's mother
nuzzles him proudly...

...as he struggles to his feet.

He spreads out
his wobbly legs,
to keep from
falling over.

Then he reaches under his mother's tummy
and starts to drink her warm milk.

A few days later, Pepper goes outside
for the very first time.

He's not sure if it's safe,
so he stays close to his mother.

But curiosity soon
gets the better of him.

He snuffles a passing butterfly...

...and peers into
shiny puddles.

In the warm summer days that follow,
Pepper makes friends with some other little ponies.

They love to race and chase
each other across the sunny meadow.

Tom and Rosie visit
the ponies every day.

Pepper learns to come
when they call his name.

Sometimes they lead the ponies into the stableyard...

...and brush their coats until they shine.

Pepper is growing up fast.

But he's not old enough
for anyone to ride him yet.

He still has lots to learn.

The children’s dad teaches him with long reins.
He moves the reins to ask Pepper
to go or stop or turn.

One day, the farrier comes
to give Pepper his first shoes.

He lifts the pony's feet, one by one,
and fixes the shoes onto his hooves.

Pepper needs the metal shoes
to protect his feet on lanes and roads.

Now Pepper is ready for Tom to ride him.

Having someone on his back
feels rather strange at first.

But Tom is patient and gentle,
and Pepper enjoys their rides.

They go exploring
all around the countryside.

When Rosie is old enough,
her dad teaches her to ride.

Pepper is patient and gentle with her.
He walks slowly until she can balance.

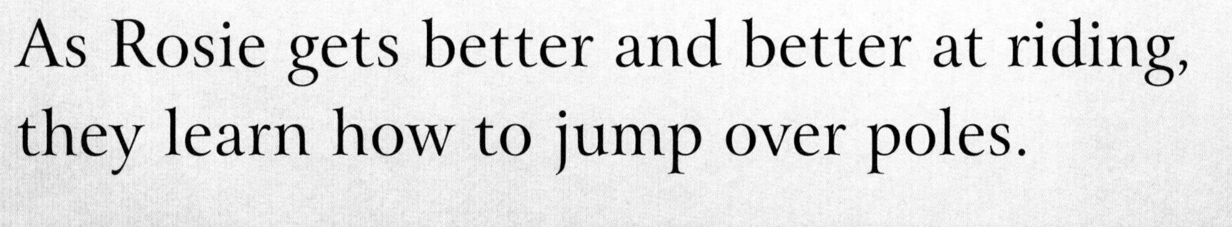

As Rosie gets better and better at riding,
they learn how to jump over poles.

One day soon, they'll be
a winning team.